THE CHONCHON MONSTER

By David Evans

Table of Contents

Jack looked down at his son, Tyler, asleep in the passenger seat of the car. It had been a long journey, and the excitement of the event had eventually worn him out. Jack had split with his wife last year, and in the divorce, she had taken Tyler.

It wasn't that Jack had tried to take him, but he was still limited by Elaine to only see Tyler during the holidays.

It had been a long time and to make the occasion special, the lonely father had booked a cabin way off grid in a forest that he had found online.

Perfect for alone man time with his son. So here they were, on the adventure of their lives for two weeks of the summer holidays.

The sun was setting by the time the pair turned onto a dirt road, that wound unevenly through a forest. The trees blocking out what little light there was, so it appeared to have just jumped to midnight.

A deer peered at them as the car bounced over small holes or pebbles along the road, the sound of birds filled the air.

As they fluttered from tree to tree, looking for their nest, or a branch to settle in for the night, away from other predators.

The cabin appeared from nowhere, it was a log cabin. That first appeared as though a giant dark hole in the middle of an already pitch-black area up ahead, it was so dark that even the car headlights seemed to struggle with piercing through. Tyler woke up as the car engine died, and Jack smiled at him, as he opened the door and climbed out. He groaned as he stretched his legs, trying to get some feeling into them.

It hadn't been a bad drive, but it was around eleven hours with only stops for lunch or to use the bathroom.

Chapter 1: Settling In

Inside the cabin was surprisingly nice. It had working electricity and looked as though it may have only recently been built.

It had a fresh, pine smell to it, with two leather sofas in the middle of the main room. Tyler sprinted across the room and opened one of the doors, then backed out and ran into the door a few feet to its right.

"My room" Tyler called out, as he dragged his bag through and closed the door behind him. Jack smiled as an answer.

There was literally no point in saying a response, as knowing his son. He would have already put his earphones in and was unpacking his bags.

As a confirmation, a high-pitched voice started coming from the other side of the door, way off tune to whatever song the boy was trying to sing, but at least he was happy. Switching the television on, that hung on a wall in front of the sofas. Jack got set on lighting the wood fire in the corner of the room.

Perhaps it was because it was nightfall, or because the trees took a lot of light from the sun, but the cabin was cold.

It wasn't long before he too found his room through the first door his son had checked. A pretty simple room at best, it had a small double bed under a window. A hanging light with no shade around it, with a wardrobe and chest of drawers.

There was a loud bang, then running footsteps. Jack blinked as a bright light hit his eyes as he opened them and tried to sit up.

"Dad, dad" Tyler jumped on his bed, "guess what?"

"What?" His father asked groggily, rubbing sleep and pain from the light from the sun shining through the window from his eyes. "Is something wrong son?"

In response, Tyler jumped back off the bed, and ran back out of the room. Being eleven years old he was showing signs of maturity, but as he watched his son. Jack realized that there were still signs of the young guy he had played catch with and gone kicking balls over the park. Who had chased pigeons along pathways and laughing as they flew away.

"Come, quick" Tyler called from somewhere in the main room.

Jack slowly climbed to his feet, put his slippers on and grabbed his dressing gown, from where it hung on the wardrobe door.

He loved seeing his kid excited, but he was still exhausted. At eleven surely the boy could entertain himself for a couple of hours before waking him up.

He eventually reached the door and peered out; the front door was open. His first thought was he was in a dressing gown and underwear, was this a prank his son was playing on him. Before he saw what Tyler was gazing at, and almost felt sick to his stomach, and blinked a few times to be sure he was not seeing things.

Outside the front door, was a stag. It was laying there, it's mouth open in horror and its eyes opened wide as if it was still trying to see.

The antlers were covered in what must have been dried blood, and a clump of fur hung from one of the protruding spikes.

The rest of the stag was almost non-existent, there was a hole in its side and all of its innards seemed to have been removed. All that really existed were the exposed ribs, curving out of the hole and back into the missing stomach.

A long trail of blood that led from the stag to the treeline, where whatever had eaten it, had evidently gone back to after its fill.

"Get away from that!" Jack ran over and pulled his son from the door, facing him away. "Don't even look at it, I'll get rid of it."

"I'm fine dad" Tyler laughed, peeking around his father's broader frame, "plus I already sent it on my Facebook!"

"You did what?!?" Jack demanded, seeing the phone in his sons' hand for the first time, "are you insane?"

"But it's so cool" Tyler said, pulling away as his father tried to snatch the now beeping phone from his hand.

That was the problem, even out here in the middle of nowhere. With the invention of data and internet phones, there was no place too isolated now.

The signal was probably low, but judging by the many sounds, it was enough to pick up everything going on with his friends and social media.

"Leave me alone" Tyler said, looking at his phone, "It's mom."

Jack sighed and buried his face in his hands. Great, just what he needed. If Elaine had seen the picture of the carcass, he was going to get into yet another argument, about being responsible. Allowing such a young boy see something that gruesome and heroic that even he felt sick, and he had grown up on a farm. Perhaps that was why he and Elaine had split up. They had been married for about thirteen years, but she was a city girl.

He was a farmer's son, who had fell in love with her during a visit to the nearest city. They had always had differences, but toward the end, they were like strangers.

They never spoke, or if they did it was an argument. He had never adjusted to city life and office work, and Elaine as much as she loved animals, hated the idea of all the work it would take caring for them.

Through the closed door, Jack could hear his son's voice, so knew he must be talking on the phone to his mother. He didn't sound upset, angry, or happy, his tone was literally conversational from the sound of it. Though the words were too muffled to really know what he was saying.

He stormed into his room, and shredded the dressing gown, and slippers, putting on his old torn jeans and a random T-shirt from the wardrobe, before stomping outside in his workman's boots. The stag was heavier than it looked. It wasn't that he was weak, Jack thought to himself as he held the antlers and dragged the body toward the trees, in another direction of the bloody trail that led into them.

It really was a big guy when it was alive, and whatever took it down, must have been extremely hungry or daring to attack such a large beast.

Though it could also have been a group of them, the fur that was still stuck to the antlers evidently wasn't part of the stags' fur, it went down fighting and probably did a lot of damage to one of its unsuspecting predators.

Jack also regretted the fact that he had left his gun at home and from what he could tell from his snooping around last night before he went to bed, they didn't leave one in the cabin for protection either.

But why would they? When he had phoned up to book the cabin, they had sworn there were no dangerous animals in the forest.

There were deer, foxes and occasionally they had seen badgers and mole hills. Other than that, the only thing to watch out for were wasp and hornet nests.

Chapter 2: Uneasiness

Evidently the guy had never seen all the animals in the forest, one had moved into the area recently.

He was lying to get the customers, though again there had never been any reviews about this. Most had been positive about it being relaxing and beautiful without any trouble.

Later in the afternoon, Jack was chopping wood, as his son watched, playing his portable game console. It wasn't really the father-son time either had planned.

The wood supply was low and if anything was to be taken from the night before, it was going to get pretty cold after dark. Tyler kept grumbling under his breath and sighing deeply, as he played the game before he finally set the console down.

"Batteries dead" he moaned, "when can I chop some wood?"

"It looks fun."

His father was just about to answer, there was a pause as he considered if his son were going to be able. The axe he found in the shed was obviously incredibly sharp and if his son made one mistake, explaining anything to his mother was going to be an incredibly difficult argument which could lead her taking full custody.

That thought was unimaginable, but the boy was eleven. So why not give him a chance, it was about time he learned some basic survival skills and took some responsibility. There was a loud scream that echoed around from the woods. It sounded like a man being tortured, but what should have killed him hadn't and he was still conscious enough to scream.

Whoever it was had definitely not seen the stag, Jack had buried it several feet underground, a long way from the cabin. Birds flew up in droves, several different species and flocked together.

Some collided with others, and others seemed to take a few moments to grab their balance in flight as they screeched and flew away from the area.

"Go inside, and lock the door" Jack demanded, as he lifted the axe over his head and stepped into the woods.

This was a dark world, it had seemed lighter this morning, perhaps it was because the sun position had changed, or because his mind was racing with all the thoughts of what might be lurking here.

Something had attacked the stag, and now there was a very human sounding scream from somewhere back here. Had whoever it was accidentally stumbled upon this new creature? Or was there something more sinister at play here?

Sweat dripped from his brow, still hot from chopping wood, but the sweat on his palms was all to do with fear. The axe slipped a little in his hands, so he gripped it tighter, though it was more for comfort of knowing it was there than stopping it falling to the floor. He wasn't an easy to scare man, he had seen things in his life. He had experienced few others while growing up on the farm, under his father's strict guidance.

Whatever it was now, it was sending a very chill shiver run up his spine. His senses told him to get out it was dangerous, and he was unequipped. His mind was on making sure that Tyler was safe and there was nothing out here, that truly posed a threat to either of them.

Plus, he had to discover what was out here sooner or later, and if it were that dangerous. At least he would meet his fate on his own terms, or at least catch this beast, or beasts off guard and kill it or them before they had a chance to get to him.

Tyler stood at the window looking out. He had wanted to go with his father into the woods and have the adventure, but whatever was out there had shaken him to the core. He had never heard a scream like that, and the look in his fathers' eyes had left no room for argument either.

He knew his father was a strong man, but he had never seen that look cross his face in his life, not even as his mother drove away, him in the back seat sobbing as his mother told him how much better their life would be.

It had been nothing but hardships, stress, and his own demons. When they had completed the divorce, Tyler had wanted to stay with his father, or at least stay in close contact with him.

His mother hated the man with a passion and never had a nice thing to say about him. Now he wished nothing more than to in that car driving away, anywhere would be better than being here.

The young man jumped as something brushed against his thigh, letting out a squeak of surprise, before it brushed against him again and he realized it was his phone vibrating in his pocket. Cursing under his breath, he pulled the phone out and looked at the screen.

His best friend Sarah, he loved her. He sometimes envisioned her as more than a friend, but he was too shy to ask her for more. He was scared that it would ruin their friendship, that it would scare her as she had always turned guys down, better looking, and richer guys than he was, and that was his biggest fear, she would turn him down and then laugh about him with her girlfriends. Clicking the red phone sign that cut the call off, he texted her quickly. His fingers dancing over the keypad expertly.

"Talk to you later, in the middle of something"

Tyler went back to looking out of the window. The phone vibrated again letting him know she replied, but he was too preoccupied to look. It had been ages since his father walked into the forest, and though he had heard no more screams nor sounds of anything other than the bird calls as they rested back on branches, it was starting to get dark. The sun was setting, and the beautiful tint of the orange sky that slowly got slightly more yellow as it approached the building spoke nothing of the fear that, was causing the boys heart to pound in his ears, or the way his heart seemed to have sunk.

Leaving him with the feeling of a freezing black hole in his chest, something dancing in his stomach and the inability to breathe properly.

Every breath felt like a struggle as it rattled in and out of his mouth, steaming the window, before the glass cleared itself.

Tyler had put the television on and was watching a Viking documentary when there was a loud thud at the door. He scrambled from under all the wrappers and snack pouches he had been eating from for the past few hours, once the sun set and there was nothing to see outside, not even the car parked a couple of meters from the window, he had given up on seeing his father again.

The police had said they couldn't locate the cabin on any map, he had no idea what the address was or even the number for the owner his father had rented from, he had never thought to ask about any of that.

It was supposed to be a nice relaxing time away, chopping wood, swimming in the lake nearby and eating marshmallows around a campfire that they would make.

Chapter 3: Worry

So far none of that had happened, except his father chopping wood by himself and leaving his son to watch.

Tyler unlocked the door, and pulled it open just a few inches. Then gasped and stumbled back holding his nose and trying no not vomit from the sight and the smell that had met him on the other side of the door.

Jack had wandered deeper into the forest than he had intended. There was nothing here though, the birds were silent, it was getting extremely dark, and he had left his torch packed away at the cabin.

He hadn't thought to pick it up and bring it as he was expecting to only chop wood then go swimming at the lake with Tyler.

In the panic of the moment, he had just rushed off thinking only of protecting his son and helping whoever might be in danger. Now he was lost, confused, and running out of daylight.

The trees around didn't help much either, they were so thick above that the light trickling in was just small beams that lit up just a few inches at a time, then it was just shadow between.

There was a low growl somewhere in the distance, which seemed to come from every direction at once.

It wasn't a loud growl, but it was one that seemed to echo and reverberate around through the trees, dancing around them.

They were even scarier than the picture he'd been thinking up about what might be back here. Who would be foolish enough to venture this deep into the forest, there was no reason.

Out of the corner of his eye, a form emerged and lunged at the stunned man who just dropped the axe and stumbled back with something incredibly heavy on top of him, causing them both to fall heavily on the ground.

Jack was winded, stars lined his sight, which was slowly returning from the dark abyss he found himself staring at. The thing on top of him groaned, it was a weak groan, as it squirmed and scrambled on top of him. Jack tried to fend the blurry outline away, before his vision finally cleared and in a beam of light, just strong enough to illuminate it, it turned out the thing was a man.

The man was balding and had a beard with only a few remaining teeth. A gaping wound on his head was leaving a bloody trail down his face that dripped onto the ground and Jacks shoulder.

"Help me" the man sighed feebly, before he flopped down, and stopped moving altogether. Jack struggled through the bushes. In one hand, he held the axe which was more of a stabilizing instrument.

His other hand was gripping the unconscious stranger over his shoulder, half carrying, half dragging him through the trees.

The birds were occasionally calling out, but otherwise, it was deadly silent. The leaves above were as still as the darkness around them. The growling had stopped minutes ago, and the air seemed to be so still, but so thick. It was like another obstacle he had to carry this man through.

Eventually they came to a clearing up ahead. It was hard to tell if it were the cabin, the road or they had gone the totally wrong direction, but there was a clearing and a clearing meant a little light, and space where he could assess everything around him.

Suddenly a flock of birds flew away, startling him and caused him to stumble over a tree root and drop the man, falling beside him.

There was a shrill *Tue, Tue, Tue* call overhead and the sound of snapping branches and rustling leaves. It had sounded like a bird, but either the bird was incredibly rare or a new species he had never heard before.

Clambering to his feet, Jack looked to where the man should be. But there was no one there. Standing up, he looked around, there was no sign of him anywhere, nothing to give away the sign of a man rolling if there was a hill there.

No footprints that might indicate he had woken up and, in his daze, and state of confusion due to the blood loss, decided to walk off and try to find his way home or something worse. There wasn't even a trail of blood, just a small puddle where the mans' head must have hit the Earth.

Slowly limping toward the clearing, axe held in his hand threateningly, Jack saw the light of the cabin window pierce through the darkness and sighed with relief. He could have cried from the weight of the burden of expecting the worse and being out of the danger of the forest.

He knew there was something lurking in there now, something that shouldn't exist. Using the handle of the axe, Jack banged on the door of the building before the adrenaline ran out and he slumped to the floor on his knees from exhaustion. In what sounded like a hundred miles away, he heard the squeak of the door open, and blinked in the light of the cabin.

There was a murmur of dismembered voices, then a scream before everything went black and nothing else mattered. Tyler had dragged his father into the cabin, then closed and locked the door again.

Blood ran down his whole torso, the axe seemed untouched by the blood, but he was more concerned that his father might be wounded or dead. The sight of his father collapsing at his feet, covered in blood had never been something he had expected in his worst nightmares, or imagined possibilities.

His phone signal was gone, he doubted the emergency services would have the ability to locate him now, it wasn't that long ago he had tried calling them before.

Jack groaned slightly, and his eyes seemed to shut tighter before going into a relaxed state of sleep again. Tyler ran to the kitchen, grabbing a cloth which he wetted to clean the blood off his father, he was alive, and the blood had dried.

So at least that meant it wasn't his blood, so what had happened out there? He had more questions than answers, but until his father woke up there was no way to get any answers. His father was also too heavy to lift onto the sofa, so he placed a cushion under his head, then started wiping the blood away.

Just in case there was a wound under it that he had missed, before getting a clean, damp cold cloth to mop his father's head with.

Seconds turned into minutes, minutes turned into an hour, then another and Jack still hadn't opened his eyes or done anything except make the odd twitch or grunt, before going silent and motionless again.

Tyler was about to give up when his father sat upright, almost headbutting him in the face. Jacks' mouth was open in a silent scream, his eyes were wide, and his pupils dilated. He had no colour, but he was awake at least, and was immediately alert.

Tyler jumped into his fathers' arms crying tears of joy. It hadn't occurred to him until now, but he had been truly terrified and worried, and all the emotions that had been kept down due to the circumstances and instinct kicking in were now flooding to the surface as he pounded his fathers' shoulder and sobbed into his chest.

> "It's okay" Jack grabbed his sons' pounding fist. His shoulder still ached from carrying the strange man earlier, "I'm okay, are you okay?"

> Tyler just buried his face into his fathers' chest harder but nodded.

"I'm hungry, how about some dinner?" Jack asked, groaning as he got to his feet.

His head was pounding, and his eyes were still a little blurry, but he felt fine otherwise. The man from the forest crossed his mind, but at this point he couldn't decide if the man was a hallucination or something real.

People don't vanish into thin air; they always leave some sort of trail behind. Tyler followed his father into the kitchen, he was still sniffing, and tears were still rolling down his cheek, but now that it was out, the anger and fear had gone too. It was as though he had had a bad dream, and just woken up.

Chapter 4: Visitor

It was past ten o' clock the next morning. Jack had slept fitfully, but Tyler was still asleep. Jack had tried to wake his son a couple of times, but he had just groaned and rolled over.

He must have been exhausted and so his father had let him sleep in. Yesterday seemed like an eternity away, yet even now, he couldn't get the man from the forest out of his head, nor the gut feeling that something was wrong.

It was as though a dark cloud formed over him and was following him everywhere. Another hour rolled by before he heard a faint sound from Tyler escaping through the door.

It was more a groan than actual speech or movement, so Jack decided his son was probably waking up and the sun had gotten him. He really needed to find something to cover the windows with at night, the light was a disaster waiting to happen. Suddenly there was a loud bang, and the sound of glass breaking.

Jack ran into the bedroom as fast as he could. Kicking the door open, he looked down at his son, laying pale in bed, his eyes were bloodshot, his long hair sticking everywhere, though the front was sticking to the sweat glistening on the boys' face. Tyler wasn't even pale, he was more a lime green than anything, and as he got closer. Jack noticed there was blood on his sons' sheet that hadn't been there the last time he came in, though he found no source for the blood, there was none to be found on Tyler's face nor clothing.

> "Dad, I don't feel so good" Tyler said feebly.

> "What's wrong?" Jack asked, sitting on the bed, and running a hand over Tyler's forehead softly.

> Tyler was burning hot.

"I don't know, I just feel weak, my body hurts, and my head is spinning" his son groaned again and sighed, shutting his eyes. "

Jack waited a few moments before thinking Tyler had fallen asleep again, so he got up to get the first aid kit he had brought and get him a glass of water for when he woke up again. He had barely reached the door though when his sons' voice stopped him.

"Where are you going?" Tyler asked, before coughing, "Don't leave me, please" he begged weakly.

"I'm not going to leave you" Jack smiled at his son, "I'm just going to get the thermometer and some water for you, just lay there and relax, son."

The smile was fake though, as soon as he left the room and pulled the door to behind him, leaving just enough of a gap to hear his son if he called out, Jack sighed and fought back the urge to scream.

Tyler had never been ill like this before, if he had, Elaine had never told him about it, and she was open about their sons' health.

Unless it was asking for more money to get Tyler clothes or new schoolbooks, she only ever called him when he was sick or injured.

He returned moments later, placing the glass of water on the counter next to some painkillers he had found in a pocket of the first aid kit.

Tyler sat up but slouched against the head stop at, resting his head and the colour drained from his cheeks again.

> "Easy, son" Jack said softly, gripping the boys' shoulder gently, as Tyler caught his balance and glanced at his father sideways.

"Here let me take your temperature, then you can take these and hopefully you'll feel better later or tomorrow. It's probably just an exhaustion after yesterday, you know worried sick isn't just an expression, stress and worry can affect people in different ways."

He slid the thermometer into his son's mouth, and waited for a couple of moments, before pulling it out and looking at it.

> "I think we need to get you to a hospital" Jack suddenly stood up and pulled his phone from his pocket. No signal. "Damn it!" he cursed under his breath, glancing at Tyler's' phone, also showing no signal. "Just what we need."

Tyler heard a noise that disturbed his sleep, groaning and feeling like he hadn't slept at all despite the light shining in the window he rolled over just in time to see a bird fly into the window.

He wasn't sure what kind of bird it was; it was large, he knew that much but he had only seen the black silhouette as it collided with the window and disappeared from view again. Before he had had a chance to react, his father had steamed in and that was when his health seemed to take a turn for the worse.

His energy disappeared, his head starting to pound, and there was a pain in the side of his neck. At first, he thought he may have slept awkward, but somehow, he knew it was a different kind of pain.

Now his dad was out shopping, there was a noise outside as though someone was creeping around the building. It was too heavy to be a bird or fox, he had never heard deer walk before but there was an instinct that told him that it was too noisy to be an animal even of that size.

Coughing and groaning, he got out of bed, and walked out of his bedroom door to find himself face to face with another man, he had never seen before.

The man was oldish looking, his tanned skin told Tyler that he was from abroad somewhere. The man was balding with a short grey stubble of a beard that looked uneven.

Tyler tried to scream and run back into the room to find something to scare the man away. At that moment, his legs gave way, causing him to fall toward the ground.

The thud and jolt of colliding with the floor never came, instead, the man had seemed to grab him in a kind of full nelson to hold him slanted, but still upright.

"Easy, easy" the man whispered, as though he were trying to calm a wild animal from a frenzy, "I'm here to help you not to hurt you."

Tyler coughed and stumbled out of the strangers grasp, the only thing holding him on his feet now, as he slowly moved toward the bed to sit on, was his own self will. The man was shadowing right behind, he could feel the warm breath on his back and smell the strangers damp, old odour.

Finally reaching the bed and sitting down, he glanced at his phone, still no signal so he could not even tell his dad to return.

So, he forced his head up and gripping the edge of the mattress for balance, he stared at the man square in the eyes.

That was his first mistake, there was something cold, hard, and merciless in that gaze from his sapphire eyes.

They weren't the dark brown he had grown accustomed to seeing in people from the Latin countries. The second mistake was trying to look brave, because in the next second, the man had grabbed his shoulder, and everything went black.

Jack jumped back in the car. The sun was hot, and he threw his shirt on the passenger seat and slammed the air conditioning on in the car.

There was no time to stop and enjoy it though, his son was ill, home alone and as worried as he had been. There was a sense of something being wrong for the past few minutes.

Chapter 5: Mateo

It had started as he queued, and the only thing stopping him from dropping everything and running out was it was all medical supplies for different things, such as the flu, mosquito bites, pain killers, bee, and wasp stings, plus so much more.

He hadn't considered that something like this would have happened though being in a forest. He cursed himself for not having the foresight of bug issues, especially ones that Tyler may have been allergic to.

Flying down the highway as fast as he could, just praying there were no police around or somebody reporting a crazy driver swerving around the traffic at speeds that made his car rattle and bounce from the smallest potholes. Jack finally spun into the dirt road, going slower, though still as reckless, almost losing control as the car slid a few times on the loose dirt and pebbles before he finally reached the cabin. The door was open, he knew he had shut and locked the door so why was it open?

Jumping out of the car, he looked around, Tyler was nowhere to be seen, he probably didn't have the energy to go into the forest, plus after yesterday, he would probably be too scared.

He made the decision to run into the cabin, and barely crossed the threshold when he saw Tyler laying on the floor in the middle of the main room, then he saw the figure looming over his son, who was laying their motionless eyes shut and drained of colour. The man had a hand on the chest of Tyler and was muttering something in a different language under his breath.

Jack ran at the man and knocked him off Tyler, before jumping on top of the man and pinning him to the ground.

> "Leave my son alone!" he demanded, adrenaline giving him more strength than he already had, "why are you here? And where did you go yesterday?" he recognised the strange man as the man in the woods.
>
> "Yesterday?" The man asked confused, "what do you mean, I was at home yesterday."
>
> "Don't lie!" Jack roared at the man, punching his cheek before pinning the man again, "you're injured, I carried you back, but when I fell you disappeared without a trace."

That was when he saw there were no wound on the mans' head, not even a mark to show he had even been cut in the slightest.

"So, he's here, after all" the man said thoughtfully, his accent suddenly thick.

Jack listened to the stranger's story, silently. The man was Mateo, from Argentina.

He and his brother were born into a family of sorcerers, only they had gone in different directions.

He had gone into helping people fight sickness and dangerous curses, his brother had gone crazy after a brawl in a pub one night and had decided that any non-sorcerer had to be dealt with and killed.

His blood thirst was so unimaginable that while most that desire to do harm go to a special kind of group, known as the Kalku, to be turned into beasts of the night. Where they can fill their blood thirst without fear of discovery, the Kalku visited his brother and turned him into what was known as a Chonchon.

Mateo said that at first, he had no idea what was going on. The Kalku turned up and demanded to see his brother.

Thinking his brother was in trouble he had tried to fight the few men who visited off but was easily overpowered. When his father had invited them in and brought his brother there, he had decided then and there he would hate them, how could his father send his own youngest son to these monsters.

They hadn't hurt his brother, Jonas, though. They had given him a vile of cream and whispered instructions to him, that his brother seemed extremely excited about. The next morning, they had awoken to his brother's body lying on the floor with no head, and the men gone.

It took years and a lot of persuasion and research to figure out his brother was not actually dead but transformed into perhaps the worst monster of all. The Chonchon could only be seen by Sorcerers and those who had a strong desire to become a Chonchon themselves, which would be the loneliest, and most gruesome life one could ever want to have. Their hearts had to truly be ice cold for them to last, it was why there were so much fewer reports in the last few centuries.

Tyler woke up, the stranger was pushing down on his chest. It wasn't heavy or strong, but it pinned him in place as though he had a mountain there. In the corner, behind the man, his dad was pacing back and forth, occasionally stopping to mutter something, then start pacing again, his eyes never leaving the man leaning over him. Perhaps he knew him, perhaps they were friends or perhaps he was a doctor he had found in town.

> "Okay, it's done" the man stood up, holding Tyler as though he were a baby, cradled in his arms, and moved to the bedroom.

"What's done?" Tyler asked, but his voice was so weak, even he barely heard himself, though the man smiled.

"Were going to make you better" he replied.

There was something odd about the bedroom, it wasn't just the night air, and the closed door blocking out the heat of the fire burning in the main room. There was a cold presence in the room, the shadows seemed darker, and the shadow of something flying in circles over the cabin roof slid past the window every time it made a pass. At one point Tyler swore the shadow looked like a human face, but as he glanced out of the window there was nothing there but the rustling of leaves in the trees.

The scraping of cutlery on China came through the door, accompanied by hushed voices. Tyler did not know how long he had slept, but he did feel a lot better. His legs were still shaky, and he felt too weak to stand on his own, but his headache was gone, and he didn't feel as feverish.

"Dad?" Tyler called out, and it was stronger than he thought it would be.

Moments later the door slid open, and the face of his father entered the room, looking sullen, and exhausted, before he saw his son sitting there and the smile alone that filled Jack's face could have warmed a room itself.

"He's awake" Jack whispered to someone behind him and stepped into the room followed by the stranger.

"Ah. Good." The man felt Tyler's neck and looked at his shoulder in the dim light coming in the door. "How do you feel my boy?" he asked.

There was no time to reply though, there was another crash and the sound of breaking glass again, only this time, glass visible came in and landed on the bedsheet.

"Hijo de mil puta!" Mateo said sternly, standing up and glaring at the window, "get away from here"

"What does that mean" Tyler asked, he recognised the Spanish sound, but had never been interested in the language.

"Don't tell h- "Jack started

"I basically called him a S.O.B" the man said with a wink, ignoring Jack altogether

"Him" Jack said defeatedly. Great, first he gets ill, and some weird man tells stories about sorcerers and magic animals, now his son is learning to curse in Spanish.

Elaine will be delighted with the outcome of this trip; she hated even the slightest words such as "Damn" or anything that could offend someone.

Chapter 6: Madness

Whatever it was though, it came back, and another panel of glass blew inwards as the sound of *Tue, Tue, Tue* came through, followed by a shadow, which got lost in the shadows.

Jack swung at it before it vanished, but he was too slow. Mateo seemed to see it perfectly well though, his eyes were sharp and focused, though he looked weak in the knees and was struggling to breathe. Tyler flew out of bed and hid behind his father. His father was shaking, he didn't look like it, but as he held his father, Tyler could feel it very easily.

"There's one way to get you away and back home" Mateo glared into a shadow, "you can only feed on them if they sleep, so we'll just have to keep them awake."

Mateo sounded a lot braver than he felt. This was the first time he had seen his brother properly since the night he thought the Kalku had killed him, after finding the headless body the next morning.

The sight of him was even scarier than the legends of the beast had described, he was a human head, part of the spinal cord came down into a sort of tail, the ears had extended and formed feathers that acted as wings.

The part of his neck that had slightly healed after the removal from the body, sprouted two taloned feet, each looking incredibly sharp.

He had led the father and son to the main room, and behind them, he heard the flapping of the wings beating against the head with a very irritated hiss.

The creature was going to follow them and going by the pair in front of him. He knew they were already on their last legs.

The fight and flight instinct draining them of what little energy they had, plus the boy had already lost a lot of blood from when the creature had first found him last night.

It was about one o' clock in the morning when he realized both the father and son were asleep and he was alone watching the movie on television.

He cursed and spun round just in time to knock the beast away from the son, and leap to his feet. He had sat between the two so he could better protect him, but it was also a hindrance, he had to get up and wave awkwardly as the bodies pressed tight against him.

He had turned too late though, as he found solid footing and was about to cast a spell at the winged beast, the last thing he saw were the hooked talons that connected with his eye. Mateo screamed and grabbed at the foot in his eye.

It was stronger than it looked and easily pulled away, leaving a searing burning sensation, followed by warm fluid running down his cheek.

Jack had fallen asleep, he didn't know when, but as the sounds of the television came back to focus, he saw a chunk of the movie had passed. He sipped more coffee before everything went dark and peaceful again.

He knew he wanted to wake up, he knew sleeping was bad, but it was so peaceful. His brain told him to wake up, it was too dangerous, but his body just refused to cooperate with it.

Then there was a sharp movement, a jolt, followed by an inhuman scream. Jack was shocked awake and looked at his son who was still asleep, fallen on his side, his head where Mateo's lap should have been. Then he saw something that would scar him forever, Mateo was wrestling with something then his eye just popped out of its socket. Retinae hung in thin air behind the floating eyeball, before it vanished in thin air. Mateo was standing there holding his eye, blood running down his cheek.

Jumping up, he led Mateo to the kitchen to give him bandages from the first aid kit. He had been prepared for cuts and grazes, but he had no idea how to deal with an eye being pulled out of a face. In the rush and panic, he threw antiseptic into the hole, which caused Mateo to scream out again, and glare with his one eye.

"Go get Tyler" Mateo screamed at him at last, "don't leave him alone, asleep with that monster."

Jack suddenly remembered and ran back to the main room. Tyler was groaning in his sleep and losing colour from his cheeks. If anything, he looked worse than he had yesterday as he grabbed his son and tried to lift him. There was suddenly a burning sensation on the father's cheek, he touched the spot to find blood oozing from a wound.

Mateo stumbled into the room too, waving a broom handle at thin air, around Jack and Tyler, shouting words and almost hit Jack multiple times who just managed to duck out of the way of the makeshift weapon.

Without thinking, Jack picked his son up and ran outside to him. Mateo called out protests that it was what the Chonchon wanted, there was more places for it to hide, and less places for them to protect themselves, especially without the gift of sight to it.

Jack was in full panic mode, he knew two things, the first was that his son was in danger and needed to be saved, the second thing was his car was parked outside, and was the fastest way out of this situation.

But as he approached the car in the darkness, he saw that he really had made a grave error, the windows were cracked completely. There was no way he could drive like that, there was no way to see out of the car and leaving the side window down to lean out of the car was going to put Tyler into more danger, there was no way of knowing if this thing, whatever it was could enter cars.

There was a loud screech and Mateo dived at the father, holding his son, and all three fell to the ground. Mateo was even scarier looking than the monster though, his eyeless socket was now hidden by charred flesh, which smelled almost as bad as it looked.

Mateo chased after Jack, trying to get him back in the cabin. At the same time, he was waving his broom at the creature again, trying to keep it from following them out. Eventually he had left an opening which the creature feinted a dive at his other eye, and when the old man was foolish enough to protect it, it had flown off in a shriek of pure malice and anger. It was then Mateo had felt dizzy, he was safe as Chonchon would rarely drink from a sorcerer, their blood did nothing for it, and could potentially be harmful. The blood loss was still a factor that if he didn't stop the bleeding. There was only so much magic he could use before he lost consciousness, perhaps to never wake up again.

He saw a poker for the wood fire, and scrambled for it, putting it in the flames for a few minutes, hearing Jack cussing about windows.

Glancing out the cabin window, he saw the Chonchon circling overhead, with his better vision, the sorcerer could see the car windows were cracked as though a tree had been swung at each one, there was not a window left untouched. The poker was glowing red now, so he pulled it from the flames, and pressed it against his eye.

There was a sizzle and a disgusting smell, it was as though someone had burned rubber. Then put old cheese on it, the pain was just as bad, gritting his teeth and holding the broom handle tight enough it started to crack in his grasp, was all he was able to do to not scream out.

Chapter 7: Action

That was when he realized what was happening. He ran out of the door of the cabin, against his better judgement and launched himself at the pair of humans standing like deer in headlights.

He collided with them, as something sharp tore through across the top of his head. Tyler had been enjoying the movie. Now something was weird, the world was black, he felt a jolt as he landed on something both hard but soft, with another weight on top of him.

In the distance he heard loud shrieks and hisses, and the flapping of hundreds of wings. Opening his eyes, he saw his father beneath him, Mateo on top of him, and blood dripping everywhere.

He turned his head and screamed in horror, what was supposed to be an eye was now flesh that was melted and fused with the skin below the eye. It was still steaming slightly too.

The smell made Tyler throw the old man off and roll over to puke on the ground, he was surprised he had anything to bring up after a day without food. Jack stood and lifted his son with him.

Tyler felt dizzy again, whatever had happened, he had slept through it, but he felt just as bad, if not worse than the day before. The car was broken too, how had he missed all of this? What was going on? Jack stumbled toward the cabin. Tyler weighed double what he had when they had first come out here, he was sure of it.

He was carrying him, but now he had patches of sick on his arm, a crazy man who was bleeding everywhere and had somehow made a gruesome sight, even more horrific.

So perhaps he was a sorcerer, how else did one make a horrible wound look a thousand times worse? Questions for another day. He lay Tyler on the sofa who had fallen asleep again, and headed for the door, to find Mateo.

He didn't trust Mateo, but whatever was going on, Chonchon being real or fake, or the old man being insane. There was something out there, and the old man was too injured to fend for himself.

"Shut the door, don't worry about me" Mateo called as he heard the man approaching. "I'll hold him." Jack grabbed the axe from beside the front door, and shut the door, locking it as he did anyway.

"Two are better than one" He called, "I don't know who or what you are, or what the hell is going on here, but I won't let my son get hurt any more than he has already been."

"You're a stubborn fool" Mateo said and grabbed the axe.

Jack let go of the axe in surprise, then tried to get it back off the old man. He was a lot stronger than he looked.

"Go inside, let me deal with this monster" Mateo said again, swinging the axe at thin air, and almost cutting the other man's nose off in the process. "He's my problem, I can see him, let me deal with it."

"Fine" Jack hesitantly agreed, he had no weapon now anyway.

He turned away to walk back to the house, when he felt pain shoot through the back of his head, and the world went dark.

In the distance he thought he heard laughter, but then there was nothing but peace and darkness. Tyler had woken on the sofa, and despite how bad he felt, he went to the window. He heard his father and Mateo arguing about something, though he couldn't see them. Then he heard a loud crack and something on the ground, followed by the laugh of something insane.

Perhaps it was the monster, it was too strong and evil sounding to be Mateo who was soft voice and definitely too wounded to laugh at anything.

But he ran to the door and opened it, finding strength in his fear of trying to find his father, and discover what had happened to him, and figure out what the noise was.

Finding his father lying motionless on the ground and Mateo standing there, axe in hand, looking in the sky above the roof of the cabin. Tyler turned his back on the old man, though he had to get an answer.

> "Who did this, what happened?" he asked, scanning the spot over the cabin his new friend was looking at, knowing he would be safe as long as he was near him.

> "I did, I'll need a snack when I turn too" Mateo said quietly.

Tyler thought he misheard Mateo, but still he turned to face him stunned before something sharp gripped his hair and lifting him, slammed him headfirst into the trunk of a large tree causing he world to go black again.

He groaned and tried to stand before collapsing in a heap on the ground. Mateo smiled at his brother, who was perched on a tree branch.

They both shared a laugh as the unsuspecting father let his guard down and was now lay crumpled on the ground.

> "He's mine" Mateo declared, "you can have the boy."

Not long after the door opened and the boy emerged, approaching Mateo. Both had perfect vision due to the magic flowing through their bodies. So, he could see how scared he was, walking slowly in the dark, already weak from the blood he had lost.

Mateo turned to the boy, his back to the creature still perched in the tree and looked up as though he was watching something there.

The plan worked and Tyler followed his gaze, asking questions, before Jonas had flown up and around, grabbing the boy and throwing him into a branch.

It was overkill, but the story about his brother was true, his brother was more bloodthirsty, than any dark sorcerer had been in the past few centuries. Suddenly, Mateo felt his neck go numb and ice cold before his legs gave way.

Chapter 8: No Way Out

Jonas had gone to his human form, and taking the axe out of his paralyzed hand, chopped down, removing the body from the head.

It was a clean cut, and very painless, there was slight discomfort as the sorcerer felt his eye rip apart. His sight slowly returned to the empty socket, before he felt a new eye in place of the old one.

That was the pleasant part though, he screeched in agony. An inhuman more beastly hiss of a scream, as the bones in his ears snapped and regrew, over and over. As the itchy feeling of something growing out of them ripped through what were now wings, three times longer than his ears had been, and a hook at the edge of each one. His spinal cord was pinned back too as skin grew beneath his chin, talons extending out, and lifting him from the ground.

Jonas watched his brother go through the transformation. It seemed much more painful than when he did it, though the people who helped him, had done it when he was asleep.

They had warned him that doing it to someone awake was dangerous, but he wanted revenge on his brother for hitting him with the broom a few times. It hadn't hurt, his skin was so thick, it was like rock, but the implication stood. There was a bonus to being asleep too, it had happened to him in a dream.

When the cream was rubbed on his neck, and after they had eaten dinner. Jonas had been given some powder to help him sleep in case he had had second thoughts or tried to do it awake.

He took it willingly and happily he fell asleep. He dreamed he was a bird, soaring high in the sky, looking down on the surrounding village, everything seemed so much clearer.

He had felt so much stronger, it was surprising. When he awoke, he was alone in a forest, a winged head with talons. The brothers drank the blood of their victims before placing them in their beds in the cabin.

They didn't want to kill them, not just yet anyway. They would be great food for the rest of their vacation.

Then they could head to the next isolated village on their way back home, each playing their game of cat and mouse with the cheery locals.

Being twins was a good and a bad omen for any of them. One thing was for sure though, Jack was the only one who had heard Jonna's calls.

Which meant Tyler was the one they would kill, before they finally left the family alone. Jack woke early, the sun was up, and Tyler was watching television.

There was no sign of the blood or struggle of the night before. He rubbed his head, it was pounding, but there was no wound there.

"Morning" Jack said waving his hand and grabbing the kettle, "sleep well? I had the weirdest dream"

Jack and Tyler spoke of their dreams, surprised at the similarity. Jack laughed and put it down to the strange location and their imaginations playing tricks on them. Surely, dreams weren't reality, though he had a sinking feeling.

The car was fine as well, no shattered windows. The tires were fine, in fact, the only issue it had was the fact it was low on gas. Which was no big deal, the town was only a couple of miles away.

The father and son were packed up and the car was packed up. Elaine had wanted Tyler home a few days early as he had been showing signs of a fever, which no matter what medication Jack gave him, it seemed to have no effect. It was a shame because it had been an idealistic holiday otherwise.

They had played ball, swam in the lake, even made a raft out of some fallen logs. They used it to paddle to the centre of the lake, and fished there, surrounded by ducks. But Tyler's health had declined to the point he couldn't stand.

As they drove along the motorway, Jack heard a strange bird call. It sounded familiar, yet so strange to him. As he watched Tyler laying on the back seat, fast asleep.

Perhaps it had been him making a strange noise, he had been struggling to breathe and perhaps he had been wheezing slightly.

Then it happened, the car jolted and flipped over, Jack held his hands over his face, protecting it from the glass flying in.

Tyler flew over his head though and out the now empty front window frame. Jack tried to reach for him, but his hand was smashed by the side of the window.

When the car finally rested upside down, Jack saw his son laying in the middle of the motorway, as motionless as he had been on the back seat of the car.

He lost consciousness too, to the sound of screeching brakes and car horns that seemed to come out of nowhere.

Neither Jack nor Tyler was ever found, the police sent a search party for them, but no bodies were ever recovered from the wreck of the car or the road.

They spent several months trying to find the pair, using dogs, using posters and television advertisements, though they would never resurface.

Mateo and Jonas had decided that the pair should rest together and carried them off to their hideaway.

www.ingramcontent.com/pod-product-compliance
Lightning Source LLC
Chambersburg PA
CBHW061729130726
47996CB00006B/2568